Gay Story and Love

Lady Marion

REUNION

I felt something tickle my balls, and with a start, I jerked awake. "Mmph!" somebody groaned, and as I sat up, I noticed I would just shove my dick an in. into a girl's throat. She took it sort of a trouper, gagging only slightly and keeping her head down, breathing heavily through her nose until I pulled back. Then she resumed rhythmically pumping my shaft in her hands and sucking on the mushroom head as if I'd never interrupted her.

My eyes fluttered for a quick second, giving me only enough time to ascertain the golden blonde head arising and down in my lap before my heavy eyelids closed themselves. the primary thought into my head was the image of a young woman's face, astonishingly beautiful. Her eyes were a golden hazel and her smile so perfect that I wanted to fall crazy together with her initially sight. The reconsideration to enter my head was that everybody else who saw this face also fell crazy together with her initially sight. and since of this, i used to be getting to need to get in line like every other poor schmuck gawking at her during this magazine.

Only I did not have to attend in line. This was no magazine; the lady in question was really here, live and within the flesh. and in contrast to all those schmucks who had only come to understand her from those magazines, I'd known her since we were children growing abreast of an equivalent street in Orange County

Back then, she'd become one among the primary objects of my concupiscence . She'd been the girl nearby , the most well liked babe in class , and therefore the head cheerleader all rolled into one. She'd been my first crush, a minimum of within the teenage sense of ohmigawd-I-sooo-want-to-have-sex-with-her. And our lives together since had progressed through sex, betrayal, love, and even family.

Cracking my eyes open once more, I stared down the length of my naked torso until my vision focused. And that I found that a stunning supermodel lusted after by the bulk of males across the earth was the one giving me this exquisitely wonderful blowjob.

"Morning, Tiger," Adrienne Dennis crooned after popping off my prick. She lapped at my cockhead sort of a kid with an frozen dessert cone a couple of times before picking her head to resume her up and down bobbing motions. And she or he hummed happily while caving in her cheeks to offer me even more intense suction. "Unnnghh..." I groaned rapturously, lifting a hand to caress her hair. She smiled around a mouthful of cock, giving me a couple of more strokes before pulling away one last time then pushing herself upright.

The goddess of sexuality who had shared my bed last night was still naked but a black leather choker with the words "Tiger's Pet" stitched into it. Her massive 36F tits were capped with erect pink nipples that jutted out from her heavy and yet firm mounds that appeared to defy gravity. I let my hands wander upwards to caress those globes and tweak their pink peaks while she hovered above my prick, holding me in her right and centering the upright rod at her gateway to heaven.

Adrienne closed her eyes as she slowly lowered herself onto me. She felt tighter than I remembered, although I appeared to be thinking that each time we'd been together lately. With Adrienne's self-determination to be a lesbian with just one dick in her life (mine), she really didn't get things as thick as my cock shoved into her pussy fairly often . So whenever she did manage to seek out time to go to , it always felt like i used to be taking her virginity, stretching her out for the very first time. "Unghhh ... so biiig..." she moaned.

Grinning, I reached up to understand the D-ring centered within the middle of her leather choker. The leash had been detached sometime last night, in order that it wouldn't interfere together with her comfort while sleeping. But the D-ring was fixed to the collar, and using it as a fingerhold, I suddenly tugged her body down against mine. Adrienne squealed as her chest slammed down atop my pectorals, and she or he continued squealing as I kicked my legs round her waist, bucking our bodies up and off the bed and rolling us over in order that we landed with me on top and my dick still buried nearly eight inches up her cunt. Giggling, Adrienne reached her hands up to cup my cheeks. With a sparkle in her eyes, she growled, "Fuck me, Tiger." then she gave me one among her patented nuclear kisses.

Without releasing our lip-lock, I pulled most of the answer of her, dug my toes into the mattress, and then rammed my hips forward. I felt her lungs compress and a puff of air begin of her mouth as I slammed into her. And while she fought to regain the lost oxygen, I pulled back and did it again. Over and over I pounded the busty blonde babe. She, DJ, and Brooke had worn me out last night, but it's amazing how refreshed one can feel after a full night's sleep. Any cobwebs were gone from my mind as I'd now come fully awake. And every one of my conscious energy was now focused on fucking the shit out of my supermodel   lover.

"FUCK! ME!" Adrienne chanted in rhythm with my thrusts. "HARD! 'ER! HARD! 'ER!" she added.

I grinned. After a year working full-time as America's newest supermodel, Adrienne's body was within the most perfect condition of her young life. Every inch of her was toned and sculpted into a mouthwateringly beautiful figure that was the envy of most of the fashionable world. I held her narrow waist in my hands and gripped it as leverage for my thrusts. Whenever my pelvis impacted hers, those massive tits bounced up to just about slap her within the face. and that i suddenly felt the urge to ascertain if I could make Adrienne's own breasts spank her cheeks, so I hammered her harder and harder and harder, slowing down my pace but putting the maximum amount force into each lunge as I possibly could. Unintentionally making my goal harder,

Adrienne threw her head back as she howled in ecstasy, removing her cheeks another few inches further away. But I didn't mind. It wasn't whether I won or lost my challenge; it had been what proportion fun we had playing the sport. So I nailed the buxom blonde over and once again, driving my prick to maximum depth then pulling most the answer.

And together with her legs rising up to wrap around my waist, Adrienne continued to verbally egg me on by pleading, "FUCK ME!!! FUCK ME!!! FUCK MEEEEE!!!"

"RRRRAAAGHHH!" I suddenly groaned as my orgasm overtook me, a touch bit all of sudden . I'd been so focused on driving myself harder and harder than I hadn't been listening to my ejaculatory control. No matter; I'd long ago stopped trying to use a playbook with Adrienne. With her, the sex was always better once we both simply moved with one another, doing what came naturally. it had been less mechanical, more intense, and always an excellent deal of fun. Fucking was just what we were both good at.

"AAAHHHHH!" Adrienne screamed as she felt me hosing down her insides. Her legs tightened around my waist, stopping my thrusts and trapping me at full depth within her. Her hands tightened round the back of my head, yanking my face down into the crook of her neck with those big tits squishing against my chin. And together, we made spastic humping motions while my cock continued to fireside spit wads of spunk into the rear of her womb. A long time later, the planet came back to me. It wasn't that I'd been knocked out. My conscious brain simply stopped bothering to trace the passage of your time . I'd reached some kind of Zen state of peace slumped over Adrienne's body, my nose pressed against her neck to let me inhale her sweet scent while my cock slowly deflated inside her. My brain was a blank slate, fully emptied by the blissful ejaculation. And for a couple of seconds, nothing during this world could possibly bother me.

But the instant passed eventually, and my senses became conscious of the sweat drying off my back, the fatigue in my muscles from the exercise, and therefore the stickiness between our naked bodies. Picking my head , I found Adrienne watching me with a wondrous smile on her face. And after nuzzling my nose together with her own, she gave me a fast kiss then dropped her head away with a forlorn sigh. We had a connection, she and I. It wasn't telepathy or any fantasy mumbo-jumbo. We simply had spent enough time together and reached A level of openness to be ready to read each other's mood. I could tell instantly that despite our wonderful lovemaking, Adrienne now felt a melancholy sadness. And that I could easily guess why. "You're leaving again, aren't you?" I asked quietly.

Taking a deep breath, she picked her head to seem back at me. Giving me a helpless frown, she sighed, "I wish I did not have to." I shook my head. "You do not have to. There is a spare bedroom right across the hall. Otherwise you could always just move in here with me." That last bit carried a faint note of hope on my part. Adrienne grinned, shrugging. "Sounds wonderful, actually. But it isn't realistic." She now looked apologetic. "I'm sorry, Tiger. But I've need to go. And that I don't even know when I'm getting to see you again."

"But you only came last night," I whined. "I know, I know. But I even have to." I frowned. "You know, for somebody who officially lives in San Francisco , you sure seem to be gone from the Bay Area tons ."

Adrienne's face fell, and she or he gave me a wan smile. "I go where the work is. and that is what i used to be trying to mention about not being sure when I'll see you again. I'm moving out of Felicia's apartment." I arched an eyebrow. By now, my dick had fully softened and slipped out from her saturated pussy. Sliding off Adrienne's body, I settled onto my stomach beside her and propped myself abreast of my elbows. "Moving where?" Somehow, I knew she didn't mean to a special apartment within the same city.

She took a deep breath, gathering herself before saying, "I'm occupation with Caroline. I told you about Caroline, right?" "Your new girlfriend Works at Vogue or something." Adrienne smirked. "I do not know about 'new' girlfriend. We've been together since May. But anyway, there's been plenty of labor coming my way in ny – it is the modeling capital of the planet you recognize – and it just is sensible on behalf of me to maneuver my home base there. Plus ... well ... I miss her." "Thought you missed me too" "I do, Tiger." She laughed, stroking my cheek. "I'll still be around you recognize i will be able to I just do not know how often i will be ready to swing by the Bay Area."

I took a deep breath and exhaled. "It

just seems like most are leaving me. Dawn's off on her 'sabbatical'. I burned my bridge with Kim. Bert's attached with Lynne now. And without Dawn, i do not skills things are getting to be between Gwen and Robin and me. Now, you tell me you're moving clear across the country!"

She gave me a warm smile, rubbing my cheek again. "You'll be fine. Your new academic year is starting, and this campus is filled with beautiful babes who would like to get to understand you better. I'll ask Brooke to stay an eye fixed on you, too." She giggled and threw me a wink. "And you recognize that I do not even need to ask DJ to offer you a touch extra attention." I shrugged and smiled at that. DJ sure had been extra-frisky ever since returning to Berkeley. Indeed, before she and Brooke went downstairs to their own bedrooms last night, the younger Evans girl gave me a glance that said she'd rather have stayed cuddled up by my side.

But the last item I wanted immediately was another girlfriend. I'd done the rebound thing twice already since Dawn broke up with me. Yeah, I felt lonely, but artificially plugging some new girl into the opening in my heart wasn't getting to solve anything long-term. And it certainly wouldn't be fair to someone as special to me as DJ.

Sighing, I blinked and brought my attention back to the important world. Adrienne had been watching me with a faint smile on her face while I'd been spacing out. And her smile got wider once I looked back at her. "You do not have to go away directly, do you?" "Uh, no," she replied with furrowed eyebrows. "I wanted to go to you, of course. But I came back to the Bay Area because i want to close up my stuff and plan to have it shipped to ny . I'm not in any hurry to urge started, but don't you've got class soon?" "Not until 11am on Mondays and Wednesdays. Perk of my senior schedule." I grinned, and then reached up to fondle one among Adrienne's beautiful boobs. "Can we go another time before you leave?" Adrienne's eyes glittered as her hand slid right down to pet my cock, which was already starting to show signs of latest life. "I'd like to .

THE BILLIONAIRE AND THE GARDENER AFFAIRS

This is a gay story which talks about a rich billionaire married to a young beautiful girl for four years, the rich man have desires and fantasizes about his Gardener. This include a most thrilling and explicit bisexual story. There is more to come, sit back, relax and enjoy the story.

I am Jon, a gardener in the house of a hot and rich billionaire named frank, He owned many companies and he is married to one of the youngest beautiful girl I have ever seen named Lori, she is so elegant and has curvy shape. But in recent weeks, I have been noticing some things because I am also a bi, Frank seems to have interest in me. Because he eyed me many times and exercise many other things. He came to tell me one wonderful day and told me that he liked me and he had been fantasying about me. I was shocked but he said we will talk later, when he returned from Airport, because Lori was travelling.

Frank POV

I am Frank, a friendly, distinguished hot billionaire happily married for over four years to one of the most elegant girl, her name was Lori. Lori was hot but Jon, our Gardener kept crossing my mind, I began to fantasize about fucking him hard. He's handsome and well shaped; I have been looking for a way and day to approach him. When I hear about my wife's travel, I took this as an opportunity to approach him and I knew the night will be long.

Back to Jon's POV

Lori was in her late twenties, and for the last four years or so, she had been living with this guy whose name I recognized was Frank. A tall woman with a wide frame and curves to match, Lori was extremely hot. She was strong and tall, not overweight. She had a tremendous collection of tits in tight sweaters and a luscious beach-ball ass that begged for a tongue that she regularly put on show. She was of Greek descent and was identical to the Greek woman who stars in CSI New York with these lovely flowing curls of hair. As a dominatrix, I constantly imagined her and had dropped several loads thinking about making me her slave. I heard his car horns when reflecting about this.

"Jon, right?" he said.

"Yes sir, Where's Lori tonight?" I asked him as he made his way to the living room.

"I just finish dropping her at the airport. She's gone to visit her mom for the weekend."

"Oh yes, I recall her saying that."

"I'm gonna come right to the point," he said,

pausing and staring straight into my eyes. "You like guys right?" he asked, and I was given away by my utter blushing. So here's the situation. Lori's out for the weekend, and you and I are going to spend some time together. I will tell you something like a cock, and I have a range of loads ready to give you, Frank said

I was initially surprised by his words, but by his dominant attitude, I was already so turned on that I could feel my cock hardening in my pants.

You have to do what I order you and not talk unless I ask you a question. I will not hurt you but you will do what I say. If anything gets to be too much for you, just let me know, otherwise I will presume you are in compliance. Is that straightforward?" he asked. As I sheepishly looked down, completely turned on, I bowed in his direction.

"Nice. Now that we've got that straight, you can start by heading under the table and see what I have for you."

Nobody could see us with my back to the rest of the room as I reached under the table hesitantly and felt my hands roam over the straight line of his well-worn jeans as I worked my way through his inner thigh. I said, Oh my god, as I felt the large size of his thickening cock stretching down his thigh. As I let my fingers discover the length of it squeezed between his thigh and his pants leg, this was the biggest penis I'd ever witnessed. As it stretched deep down his inner leg, I could almost feel the heavy heat from it through his jeans.

He said, "I feel it is time to get out of here and

put that nice little mouth of yours to effective use," he said, as he put his right hand in front of my face and stretched his thumb, "Now, let's see that mouth of yours," "Suck on that for awhile," and I pushed my lips down and over his thumb. I used a suction motion with love that I hoped would satisfy him. I varied my pace up and down to make it fun for him, using plenty of salt.

Aahh, that's cool. You will do just fine. Yeah, that's it... Lovely and warm... It's slow and firm... You will soon get a sweet reward. I think you're going to enjoy my cum being taken. I cum a lot when I cum, and you just make sure you're not wasting any of it, okay? I clearly nodded as I started to make love with my tongue and lips against his thumb.

I accompanied Frank into the smartly decorated space and followed him to a big master bedroom with a king-size bed in the back. Frank swung on the light switch that triggered one of the table lamps on the bedside table. Frank pulled off his shoes and socks and floundered himself into an easy chair, sitting in a corner of the room opposite the bed.

Now you can undress, boy," he directed. Labeling me "boy" just emphasized his control over me. I stripped my clothes down to my modified boxers and stood awaiting, somewhat sheepish. "All the way, and when you're done, leave your hands at your sides." I did as he told me and stood there with my 6" cock as I had alternated between being turned on and somewhat shy.

Frank said, "Stroke your cock a bit, I want to see what you've got there," I picked my cock and stroked it quietly for a minute, until it was very hard. "Not bad," Frank said as he stood up, "Come over here." I walked over to where Frank stood and my loosely formed 5'-7 seemed to overshadow his 6'-3 " wide-shouldered frame. He pulled his work shirt's tails out of his trousers and gave me my next set of orders, "You can start by showing me off with this shirt." I began to undo the corresponding buttons the front of his shirt and his broad chest came into view progressively.

From the middle of his chest, a fine layer of dark hair spread out and the definition of his pecs revealed the amount of hours he must have spent at the gym. He smelled... Well......well... The finest word I can use to describe it is manly. A bit musky, a bit sweaty, all guy. I could see his smooth, strong stomach and a fine line of hair leading to the top of his jeans as I continued to finish unfastening his shirt and peeling it away from his body.

"You like what you see?"You like what you see? I nodded and sheepishly looked down.

For the rest, you might want to kneel down, "You might want to kneel down for the rest," I got the idea and needed no coaxing, falling easily to my knees with his crotch and my face level. I saw his cock stretching down the leg of his jeans, more than halfway to his knee! His fading jeans had a damp spot where some pre-cum had leaked in.

I unfastened his large belt, pressed the button at the top of his jeans, and pulled his zipper down, revealing a nest of dark curly hair at the base of a very large dick that I could see. There was no clothing to get in my way, and he had gone commando. I pulled the back of his jeans off his good firm round ass and went on to work them down, revealing his cock more and more. Finally, it popped right into view and I just had to sit and wonder at it. It was a beauty still at around 8 'long and so wide around that I knew I probably won't be able to close my hand around it with a beautiful voluminous firmness. He was cut across the base of his large mushroom head by a very prominent ridge. Only looking at it, I knew my lips were going to find a nice home behind that cockhead lock. Frank picked his foot up and the rest of the way off, I took his pants. I knew I could worship this man all night, with his feet shoulder-width apart and his heavy cock beginning to rise. Frank put his hands on either side of my head and put them in my hair.

"Time to get to work," he said, dragging me in

his direction. I was hit all of a sudden by a different scent coming from his cock and his balls. Highly familiar, but unexpected. He took note of my reluctance. "Yes, that's Lori you taste. We just had time for a second fuck before I dumped her at the airport. I didn't have time to take a bath. Your main job is to be my cleanup boy, I guess."

Oh darn it, this was better than I'd ever dreamed! A little while ago, the lady I worked with who I had jacked off several times had just been fucked by this stud and her pussy juice was still on his dick!

Until you start working for your main course, get me nice and clean," he said as he gently patted into the easy chair and spread his legs wide in invitation. He sat near its front edge with his ass so that his huge cum-filled balls hung over the front edge with his thick cock bouncing over them towards me, the piss-hole shining with his precum. I didn't have to be asked twice and moved forward". As I extended my tongue and reached his hot cockhead, smelling Lori's sweet juices as well as his manhood, the scent was addicting. First, I bathed his cockhead, feeling it start to swell and grow as I licked him clean lovingly. I worked my way down his rising shaft, busy with my lips and tongue, getting every drop of their joint juices.

He said, "Aahh ... that's great, you certainly know what to do with a cock don't you," as he took my head in his hands again and pulled me around his cock and balls, where he needed my next action. As a sign of acceptance, I simply 'purred' and resumed my caring work. I pulled my head back until I had completely washed his cock and nuts, and then stared at his cock in utter hardness. With a fall of pre-cum in the piss-slit, the broad angry head was glowing and the thick shaft was transversed with buzzing veins. A truly strong thing about appearance.

How......how... Uh, uh...... And how large is it? 'I was telling Frank.

It's ten and a half," Frank replied, "you think you can take it all? I shuddered at the monster's idea of entering my neck.

"I think I'd like to try," I whispered softly.

Yeah, I'm trying to be gentle, but by the end of the weekend, you're going to take it all, don't worry."Oh, I'll be gentle but you'll be swallowing it all by the end of the weekend, don't you panic."

"There now, put your tongue out and get a little feel," he said as he brushed my distended tongue with the tip of his cock. I savored his pre-cum flavor, slightly salty and wet. I needed more, and with my eyes closed and a soft meowing, he could tell, like a kitten with a plate of hot milk.

That's sweet, now you've got a taste of it. Get this first load to work and you'll get a good, dense, wet reward. "I want to see it first when I cum, don't consume it right away." He sat back with that and let me go to work on his pulsating cock. I managed to reach out and yanked it forward with my hand until it was in accordance with my mouth. I opened my mouth broad and slipped the cockhead in, closing my lips behind the ridge.

"Ooohh, yes," Frank moaned as I kept satisfying him. I gently flicked my tongue all over the head of his big mushroom, becoming used to the size and feel of it in my mouth.

This was a strong cock, only in size and thickness, I could feel it. At the same time, hot, strong and pleasant, it was a beautiful tool for pleasure.

I went down the shaft a few slow inches and I was at my gag reflex when I got around halfway and drifted back to service the head. Again, I moved forward, purring and pushing with my tongue on the underneath of his cock. With some slight pressure and plenty of saliva, I repeated this over and over; accelerating and then slowing down right down to make it cool, hot and slippery for him. By the constant moans he was emitting, I could tell he was delighted with my cocksucking skills. I worshipped the cock and its splendor. I could only take around 5 or 6 inches, but at this point, which seemed to keep Frank pleased. On the lower half of his dick, I used both palms, slick of my excess saliva flowing down from above.

"Use your fingernails and lightly scratch from around base of my cock, I like that," said Frank. My nails were small, but there was a little there, and as directed by my master, I did.

"Oh, that's so good ... yeah ... just like that ... yeah ... just keep this going and I'll be having an orgasm soon."

With my diverse sucking motion, I kept working the top half of his cock and using my palms and fingernails on the lower half and base. I found that his giant balls were drawing closer to his body, and I realized that he was close to feeding me. Since we began, my own cock had been solid as a rock and I could claim I would like some release soon, but I knew that Frank's enjoyment came first.

"Oh, that's it ... yeah ... you're going to get that set soon," Frank said as he reached out, putting his hands back on either side of my head. He fondly moved his hands through my hair, leading me to his cock. With its pulsating warmth, it seemed to grow a bit stronger and bigger, and I knew that he was close.

"Oh yeah ... here it comes... ,"Oh yeah... here it comes. I wanted to ensure I swallowed his load, and I didn't inadvertently go straight down my throat, so I eased off until I locked my lips behind his cockhead's ridge. The first shot dismantled hard into the back of my mouth and he gave a slight buck. It was swiftly followed by another and another. His hot, creamy, thick cum was filling me up! He winced and gave off another volley of shots, filling my mouth quickly as he proceeded to cum and cum. I couldn't keep it all, and I seeped out the corners of my mouth a little and lowered my chin down on his cock and thigh. His load of cum began to diminish after around 11 or 12 shots. My god, I was thinking, this guy just fucked his wife a while ago, and he almost soaked me with his cum! As he fell back into the chair with closed eyes, my mouth was completely full and his cock lost a little of its hardness but still retained its strong strength as I held my oral grip on it.

His hands raced with soft caresses through my hair, letting me know that he was happy with the job I had done. Okay, back off now and let me see what you have there,"Okay, back off now and let me see what you've got there."I slipped my mouth off his cock and a few drops slipped onto his cockhead. I stared up at him inquisitively and opened my mouth. "Well, you taste good and full." "Okay, you can sip now." he put his hand on the side of my throat.

I shut my mouth and picked up my first swallow, wet and creamy with his cum as it made its way down. To get it all down, I had to swallow 3 times, Frank fondling my throat as his cum found its way to my belly. Let me help you with that here,"Here, let me help you with that," Then he put his hand in my mouth and I gave it a clean lick. He continued this before his load cleared my face. "It looks like a bit managed to get away from you. We can't have it now, can we?" he said as he took my head again and guided my lips to those drops that had missed my mouth and spilled onto his cock and thigh. I licked each drop lovingly. I just can not imagine how much cum he absolutely fed me!

He gazed at my ponderous dick, and in his chair he sat back down. "Okay, I think you need yet another little treat for being such a successful little cocksucker. What I want you to do is take my cock deep into your mouth and lick at it while you jerk off. I want you to trap your own cum in your hand and then, well, I think you'll know what to do."

Once again, I stepped forward and enthusiastically pulled his heavy monster back into my mouth and kissed and licked that massive cockhead. In my side, I took my own cock and began to jerk it off. I was so turned on, I knew it wasn't going to be long, and I had what felt like the most intense orgasm I'd ever had, after only 30 seconds. While whispering around Frank's dick, I pumped about 6 strong shots into my other side. Frank sat forward as I began to relax, and he took my cum-filled hand and placed it in front of my face.

There you go, just lick it all up and we're going to be prepared to move on to round 2 probably shortly. Under Frank's close watch, I gulped down up my own cum, not leaving a drop. It wasn't nearly as good as his cum, but nevertheless, I was pleased. I was looking forward to round 2.

I had just completed sucking my first load out of Frank and I was taking a knee in front of him after licking up my own cum, too. "Well, let's pick up a shower before round 2," he said, getting up from his chair.

I accompanied him into the en-suite bathroom with a wide shower stall extending from the ceiling to the curb on the floor with glass walls. Splendid marble lined the stall. It was one of those ones made with a nozzle at each end for two people. Frank reached in and got the water flowing and grabbed a few giant furry towels on an adjacent wall which he placed on hooks.

"I think that ought to be hot enough now," he said, stepping in. I followed after his master like a little baby and the warm spray rolling off Frank's body felt calming.

"Now we'll only bide our time on this first one but probably shortly I'll expect you to handle all my piss with no reluctance. Now open that pretty little mouth of yours and get ready." I did as he asked, and Frank gave his cock a few small strokes and kept the tip a few inches from my open mouth.

We're going here, "Here we go... ," It took me a second to get used to the amount so easily entering my mouth and some of it was flowing out and down my chin already. As his piss found its way to my stomach, I swallowed to try and keep up and was compensated with a wet, soothing feeling. Frank's cock clenched and the flow ended. With hungry eyes, I looked up at him.

"You ready for more?" he asked. As he stepped slightly away, I nodded rapidly.

"Okay, here you go..." he said, releasing the next stream of yellow liquid into my gaping mouth.

As his piss kept flowing, I swallowed and swallowed. He backed off and proceeded to shift his dick all over, streaming all over my face, my hair, and my chest. It felt like my skin was running hot and I realized I was hooked. He put his head back completely into my mouth as his stream faded and I locked my lips behind the ridge once more as I swallowed the rest of his pee. I kept breastfeeding, hoping for more, until Frank pulled his cock out of my mouth at last.

For now, it's enough. Don't panic, you can get everything that you want afterward. It's time for you to get me prepared for your next medication load,' he said, turning back to the water spray.

I took the bar of soap given to me by Frank and began to lather his back. Under his skin, I could feel the natural abilities of his rippling muscles. I made my way down his back to his bubble-ass, soft and firm. I started to run my soap-covered hands over all those huge piles, gripping and scratching. I ventured my hand into his butt as he stepped against the shower wall to open up to my ministries.

"That's good, get that ass nice and clean, "That's good, get that ass nice and clean. I made my way back to his strong legs after having spent a couple of minutes on his ass, down for the rest of his legs and eventually massaging the soap into his feet. Frank turned around to face me as I rose, lifting one of his arms. In order to run my hands around his shoulder and upper arm and into his hot moist armpit, I coated my hands in soap again and stepped closer. I grabbed my time and Frank grinned at me.

I nodded in agreement, "You like that, eh?" and grinned at him as I went about my job. The feeling of his muscular arms and body was amazing under my fingertips. I couldn't trust my luck to run into Frank as my boss

To his happiness, I must have ended on that arm as he lowered that arm and raised the other. I applied my attentions to his other arm and then made my way down to his flat belly through his strong chest. As Frank relaxed against the wall and let me have my way with him, I re-loaded my hands with water and soap and gradually worked my way down into his pubic hair. I used both hands to stroke through his pubic hair and his heavy cock around the base. I used my fingernails to scrape the thick base gently, and this prompted Frank to make another moan of joy.

'That's it, you're easy to learn what I want,' he said, placing one hand on the base of his cock and moving the other down to cup his massive balls and gently massaging them as they hang loose in their pocket. They were massive, and I couldn't keep them both in one hand. I found that under my lathering, his cock was beginning to stretch out and yet the sheer size and weight of it caused it to hang well below horizontal. I knew more publicity would bring it to its full glory later on. As I lathered the length of that massive dick, I then shifted my hands one over the other, being careful not to get any biting soap into his piss-slit.

Yeah, that's fine," Frank said. "We're ready for round 2, I hope.

We rinsed and got out of the tub.

Second, dry me,"Dry me first,"

Before even being allowed to dry myself, I grabbed the towel and passionately dried it from head to toe. Frank returned to the bedroom when I was finished, allowing me to look after myself. Frank had pulled down the duvet and sheets when I stepped back into the bedroom, and had moved a few pillows to the head of the bed. He was lying on the pillows, propped up, and when I stepped into the room he split his muscular legs with an invitation.

"I think you know where you belong..." I crawled obediently to the bed and sat between his powerful thighs, my face inches from his thickening cock. Frank took in his hand his heavy cock and raised it out of the way.

"Get your tongue down there and work on those balls for awhile," he ordered. I stepped forward enthusiastically, spreading my tongue over the wrinkled surface of the giant orbs. One at a time in my mouth, I softly manipulated them, moaning as I did so. I serviced his sack for ten minutes or so as Frank stroked his cock slowly. He kind of folded his hips and as I backed up a bit, he said, "I want to feel that nice hot tongue on my asshole for awhile." He raised his knees to allow me more access and I dived in, intoxicated by his clean asshole's warm moist scent. I moved my sweet, slippery tongue and lips lovingly around his wet pucker. On the opening, I pressed softly and felt Frank relax as my tongue made headway into him.

Affectionately, I picked it up and swallowed it, eager for more.

Frank ran his hands through my hair once more as I made love to his cock. As I closed my lips behind the ridge, making my way downwards, I was bent on taking more of him than the last time. I pulled my stretched lips farther down his cock, then backed off with a firm swirl with my watering tongue on the underside of his penis. He awarded me with his Precum's drooling gob.

I leapt forward again after swallowing the delicious teaser, bringing him deeper into my mouth. Although keeping my hands occupied around the base of that thick cock, I repeated this action, my thumbs pushing upward on the base's underside as I pushed downwards. I was able to get about 6' in, but I was concerned that if that was all I could take, Frank would be disappointed with me. Frank seemed to feel my concern and he stopped me in mid-suck with his hands on my head.

I think we need to focus on loosening your throat. I know what you need,' and he swung his leg over my head and stood on the side of the bed with it.

"Lean back and just let your head hang over the side of the bed, "Lie on your back and just let your head hang over the side of the bed. I did as he asked, and I could see that massive cock towering over my face as I looked up. Frank took his hand and bent down his dick and traced around my cheeks, lips and eyes with the dripping end of it. Everywhere he reached me, I could feel it leaving a slippery trail.

Good, I love to see my juice on your face. I'm sure you don't mind. Before we're through and, you'll get a full load there. Good, "That's I love to see my juice on your face. I'm sure you don't mind. You'll get a full load there before we're thru."

Now, just spread your big sweet mouth and try to relax that throat.' I opened my mouth wide and he moved forward, pressing down on the top of his cock so it met up with my mouth. His cockhead filled my mouth and he moved forward softly, taking it to my throat's opening. He slowed down as I gave a mild gagging reflex unconsciously.

That's all right, "That's okay, "We're just going to keep moving to this depth for a while," We'll just keep moving to this depth for a bit," He got to the same point as last time and kept it a second longer there. He replicated this over and over, at the approach to my neck, each time lasting a little longer. When he got to that point, I was getting used to his thick dick being so deep in me and was no longer gagging.

'All right, now this time I'm just going to go a little deeper, so really try to relax the throat,' he said, taking his big hands and softly massaging the sides of my neck outside my throat. I felt him change his position and then he began his forward motion, feeding me with that huge cock. When he reached the entrance, he stopped and then moved gently forward, stroking my neck softly at the same time. I focused on calming my gag reflex and then felt his massive cockhead fill my mouth with it. I've got it sorted! He backed out softly, leaving the mushroom cockhead still in my mouth. "That was very pleasant, you took about two more inches that time. I knew you can do it ... want to try for the rest?" he asked. As I kept his cockhead trapped in my mouth, I made a shaking motion with my head.

Okay, here we are again, and with that he stepped forward again, paused once again for a second at the entrance to my throat and then inched his cock harder. I felt it going further that it had last time, and he kept pushing forward, feeding it into me. My throat felt full but unscathed. With my effort, I knew I had to satisfy Frank. I felt something different on my face and realized that Frank had stopped moving and his ball rest on my chin.

"Well, you got it all, all 10 ½" That's one lovely throat you've got in there. Ready to do some long-thicks? While flicking up a load of precum with my tongue, I giggled my accord again. He moved forward again as he stretched his hips and his dick came straight down with no problems this time. He started a see-sawing movement where he would go right to the bottom of my throat and then pull back until my lips were touched by just the tip of his cockhead, then drive it forward again. He kept it up as I kept it up. I had a lot of saliva created to ease the movement of the beauty inside me. When he started to pound into my mouth, the slickness was coating his balls and thus my own lip.

He said, "I'm getting' close, real close," as he

kept pushing his big, throbbing cock all the way out and then all the way into me. On the underside of his massive cock, I felt the throbbing as he pushed to the hilt one more time and kept it there, deep in my throat.

OH FUCK... GET READY!"OH FUCK ... GET READY!" Again, jet after jet of thick, sweet, creamy cum followed. Once more, my mouth filled and Frank just kept aiming. Just from taking his load, I felt my own cock firing, my own pleasure mixing with his. He kept firing, a little less now, but still seeping into my mouth after the end of my own climax. His moans from above urged me on from his spewing cock to nurse even more. Finally, he finished shooting and there were a few dribbles that found their way into my mouth. Some of them had once again spilled out of the corners of my mouth and flowed down the sides of my cheeks with my head upside down. "Let's see what you've got there," Frank said, taking his cock absolutely out of my mouth. He looked down at my mouth, which was almost overflowing with his sperm.

That's pretty... I knew you wouldn't want me to deny you the satisfaction of firing straight into your throat and tasting it. Okay, go forward with and swallow,' he said as he put his fingers next to my throat again to feel his cum going down. To get it all down, it took me another three devours. I could believe a nice warm coating of his cum in my mouth, throat, all the way down to my stomach as I kept flowing through a pleasant sense of pleasure and contentment.

As he stretched out with his fingers and scooped up the leftover cum from my cheeks that had leaked out, he said, "Looks like you missed a little again," He put his fingers in my mouth to give me a clean lick. He brushed his fingertips over my stomach after he had done with my face, and carried the remnants of my own load to my mouth. Every drop which seemed to satisfy Frank, I licked up. That's good, you got off on me for a long time, thickening your throat. You had a pretty decent load for a little tpleasure. I had moved back up fully onto the bed and was laying sideways on it recovering from my latest ordeal of pleasure

Well, that's a good weekend start. Are you up for more?"Well, that's a good start to the weekend. Are you up for more?"It's a good start. I nodded swiftly and smiled. That's good. I think I would like your tongue back in my asshole for a little while, "That's good. I think I'd like that tongue of yours back in my asshole for a little while," I had a great view up into his ass's crease and his little pink anus. Slowly, before I extended my tongue and rubbed it over that hot hole, he lowered himself.

"Oh yeah, that's good. Get that tongue in there," he said, settling down in a comfortable Place on my face at the end. He rode my face for 15 minutes or so as I kept tasting, kissing and licking with my lips and tongue. Once more, Frank was stroking his cock as I worked on his anus. I couldn't believe this man's stamina! Only a few hours ago, he poured one load on his girlfriend and then just finished feeding me two huge loads! Eventually, he climbed away from me and settled back, leaning against the headboard pillows. He pulled his knees up and separated his legs once more. He pointed at me with his tough 10 1/2" at me and said, "Here you go. Again, I have something good for you.

From my work on his butt, his cock was rock hard and I shifted between his legs. I took his cock's head into my mouth and it felt like I was back home again, in the place where I was supposed to be. Frank moved his hands off his cock and guided his huge rod up and down my head. As I went up and down on his pulsating cock, I used my hands again, scratching and swirling at the base. I noticed from this place after the long-thicking session that I was able to take a little more than before, probably close to 8.'

I varied my sucking speed and then I would take my mouth off completely to lick up and down the sides. Under my ministers, Frank started to whine and once again he was continuously feeding me a drooling mass of precum. For about 20 minutes, I kept this up, keeping it just on the verge of orgasm. Okay, now I need to cum,"Okay, I need to cum now," Lay down on those pillows with your head," Lay down with your head on those pillows," In line with my mouth, Frank straddled my chest and forced his cock back down. He stepped forward with his hips and fed it to me. He used fast, quick strokes as he kept his head back and fucked me in the ass. As he saw himself in my mouth back and forth, I felt the strength of this man and his immense throbbing cock.

Oh fucking... He shouted, and then as he pulled his cock out of my mouth, I was surprised. I looked up just as he wrapped his hand around his cock and milked it quickly as he pointed it directly at my face while holding it with his other hand on the top of my head. I saw his piss-slit seem to flex and then the first huge shot of cum fired on my face, hitting me just below the eye. This was followed by another giant shot in the nose and upper lip that struck me square. Frank proceeded to pump on my face with his cock and direct shot after shot. The loads were unbelievable from this guy! Again, there had to be eight or ten wide shots of his hot cum covering my face. I've been a mess... Yeah, but oh so happy.

Frank ended up sticking his giant cock back into my mouth to finish taking his last drops of cum for me. I nursed the beautiful cockhead again, which proceeded to feed me with his life-giving juice. "He eventually knocked back and looked at me. "With my cum all over you, you look great. I can hardly see what you look like. I know where you want that load here," he said as he approached over to the side table and snatched a spoon that was there. He used a spoon to scoop my face with cum and feed it to me. He repeated this until, where I needed it, I had his entire load inside me. I enjoyed every drop and cleanly licked the spoon. He's a nice kid. This weekend, you'll be doing just fine.

I was curious what Frank had planned next for me...